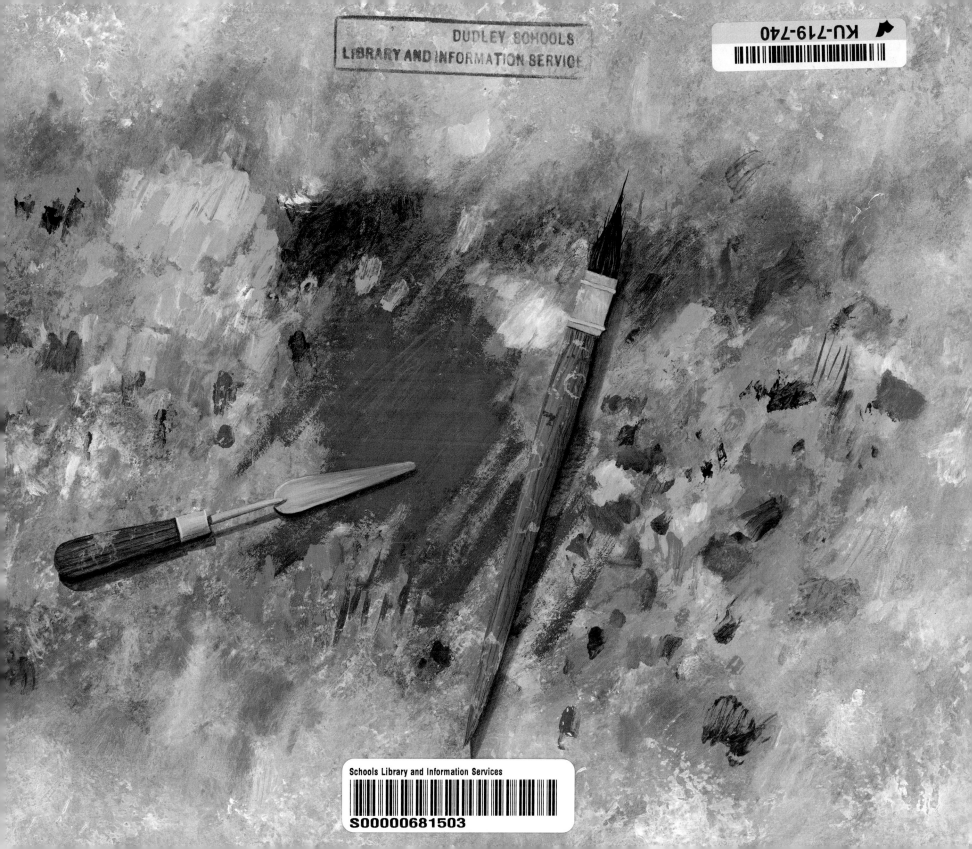

For my grand-daughter, Coco.
—JW (13.11.2006)

Little Hare Books
8/21 Mary Street, Surry Hills
NSW 2010 AUSTRALIA

First published in 2007

National Library of Australia
Cataloguing-in-Publication entry
Winch, John, 1944- .
Fly, Kite, Fly! : A Story of Leonardo and a Bird Catcher.

For children.
ISBN 978 1 921049 81 1.
ISBN 1 921049 81 2.

1. Leonardo, da Vinci, 1452-1519 - Juvenile fiction.
2. Bird trapping - Juvenile fiction. 3. Birds in art -
Juvenile fiction. I. Title.

A823.3

Designed by Serious Business
Produced by Phoenix Offset, Hong Kong
Printed in China

5 4 3 2 1

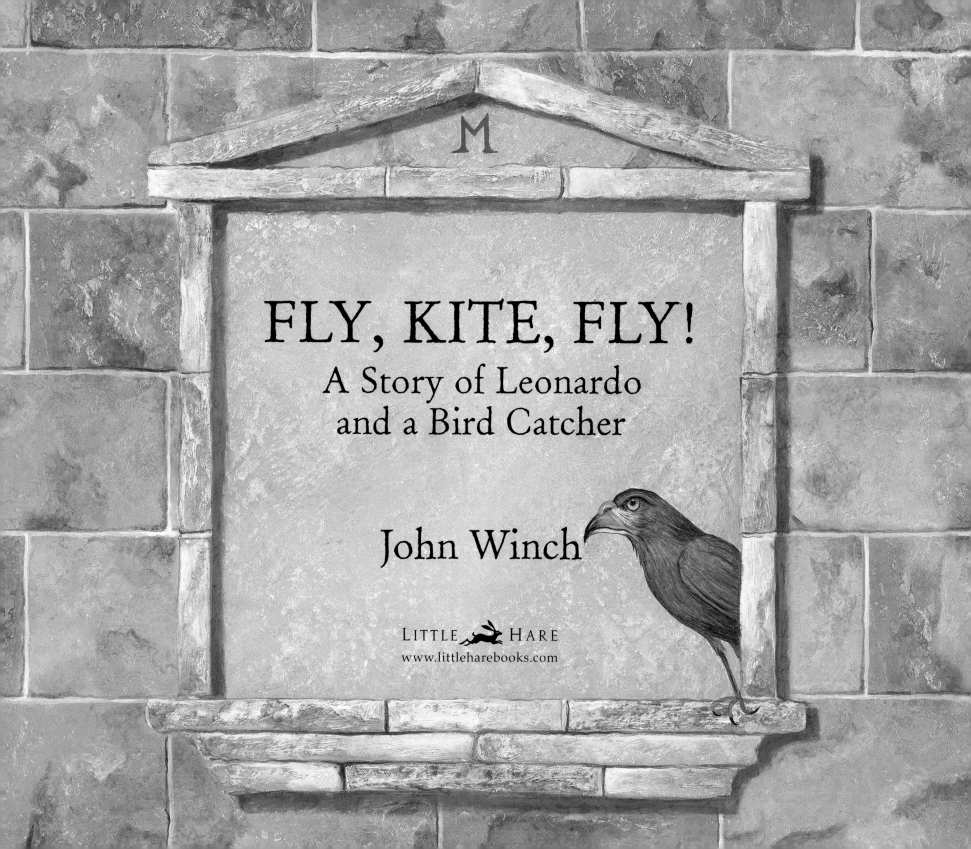

FLY, KITE, FLY!

A Story of Leonardo
and a Bird Catcher

John Winch

LITTLE HARE
www.littleharebooks.com

Giacomo longed for the day when he would become a bird catcher like his father. But his father had other ideas.

"You have to study and become a scholar," his father said. "The life of a bird catcher is hard, with very little reward."

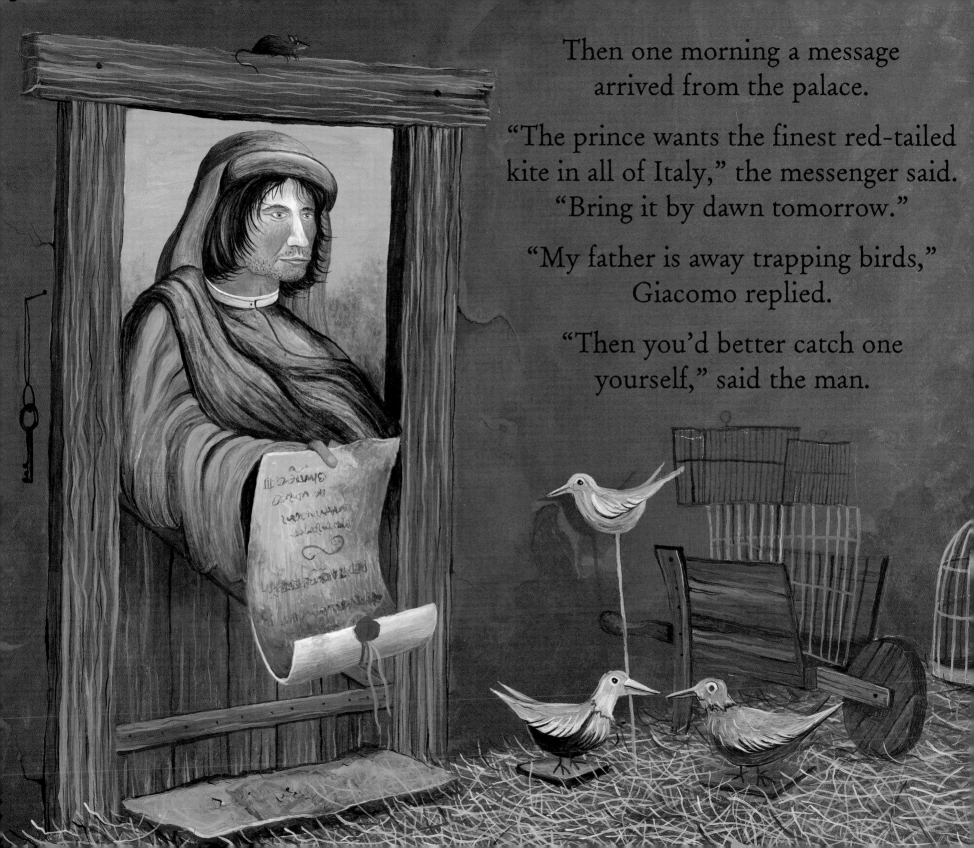

Then one morning a message arrived from the palace.

"The prince wants the finest red-tailed kite in all of Italy," the messenger said. "Bring it by dawn tomorrow."

"My father is away trapping birds," Giacomo replied.

"Then you'd better catch one yourself," said the man.

This was Giacomo's chance to prove himself. He gathered his father's old nets and traps and set out into the fields.

First he searched the meadow that surrounded the town but there he found only ravens.

He ran to the river... but found only herons.

Giacomo set decoys… but they didn't seem to work.

There was nothing in the traps he set…

...and all his nets were empty.

Giacomo worked all day. He searched high and low.

But he couldn't find a red-tailed kite anywhere.

When dusk fell, there wasn't a bird to be seen.

In despair he prepared to head home.

Then something caught his eye.
It was not one red-tailed kite, but two!

"Wait!" cried Giacomo. "Stop!"

But it was too late. He had frightened
the birds away.
Then Giacomo saw something else.

"Whose kite is this?" Giacomo
asked the old man.

"It's yours if you have a use for it,"
he replied. "I have launched it from
the highest tower, and it
glides like a bird."

Together they worked
through the night...

Giacomo arrived at the palace just as the sun was rising.

In his hands was the finest red-tailed kite in all of Italy.

The prince rewarded Giacomo with coins of silver and gold. The prince knew how precious the kite was—he could see it had been created by Leonardo da Vinci, the greatest living artist of the day.

As for Giacomo, he finally got his wish to become a bird catcher. But instead of trapping birds in cages, he became Leonardo's friend and learnt to capture the likeness of the birds on paper.

Author's note

Leonardo da Vinci was born in Vinci, Italy in 1452. He was the son of a lawyer. He died in Amboise, France in 1519. According to legend, the king of France wept by Leonardo's deathbed, saying that "no man has ever walked this earth who knew as much as Leonardo da Vinci".

Leonardo's journals about art, drawing, anatomy and invention show us that the king of France was probably right. Leonardo da Vinci was in many ways centuries ahead of other artists and inventors of his time. Unfortunately, after he died, his journals disappeared. By the time they were eventually found, hundreds of years later, modern inventions had taken over and left Leonardo's inventions behind. Even so, most of his ideas have been proven to be right, and all his inventions would have worked if he had been able to build them.

There are many books about Leonardo da Vinci and his life and work. But what has interested me the most is Leonardo's meeting with the boy who became his life-long friend and companion. Nothing about this meeting is known except that they met on the Feast Day of Saint Mary Magdalene in 1491, and that the boy was ten years old. The story of *Fly, Kite, Fly!* is my way of imagining how this meeting might have taken place.

—JW